WALT DISNEP
Robin Hood

Twin Books

GALLERY BOOKS
An imprint of W.H. Smith Publishers Inc.
112 Madison Avenue
New York, New York 10016

"Top of the morning to you! Allan-a-Dale's the name, and I'm a wandering minstrel. I keep my eye on things around here. Let me sing you a song about the good folk of Nottingham town and the great forest of Sherwood, home to the most famous hero that ever lived, Robin Hood, and his band of Merry Men."

Listen carefully now . . . The big brown bear's name is Little John and the sly fox by his side, why that's Robin Hood. To some these great pals are bandits, but to others they are heroes, for they have only one crime: robbing from the rich to give to the poor!

Our story begins with Robin and Little John together in Sherwood Forest, roaring with laughter. Suddenly they heard a rumbling noise.

"Quick, Little John! Let's hide. It might be the scheming Sheriff and his posse," said Robin.

The two friends were astonished to see a magnificent golden carriage passing through the clearing.

"Wow!" said Little John, "I thought King Richard was away fighting in the Holy Land."

"The imposter riding in such style is his brother, Prince John," explained Robin. "But luckily for us, he is even sillier than he is wicked. Hurry, Little John, I have an idea."

Robin and Little John darted behind some trees, and reappeared moments later, gaily dressed as gypsy women. Robin hurried after the royal coach and Little John followed, hitching up his skirts as he ran.

"Stop! Stop!" cried Robin. "Fortunes forecast . . . luck charms. . . . Let us show you what riches await you."

Inside the royal coach, Prince John was admiring his reflection.

"Oh! S-s-sire, how regal you look," admired Sir Hiss, the snake.

"Yes, Hiss. Beneath such a jewel my noble head . . ." began the Prince.

". . . is even more noble than King Richard's," interrupted Sir Hiss.

"Silence, silly serpent!" commanded Prince John. "Never speak my brother's name. You will hiss no more today." And with that, the wriggling reptile found himself locked in his basket.

"Halt!" cried Prince John when he heard the gypsies. He could never resist having his fortune told. "Step inside," he said to the friends.

Hiss suspected a trick and hissed louder than ever when Robin stepped inside the coach, but the Prince gazed lovingly into the crystal ball. He did not notice the sack of gold Robin pulled away from Hiss!

13

Robin fled from the carriage laden with gold, stopping only to grab Prince John's ermine cloak.

"Stop thieves! I've been robbed!" yelled the furious Prince, realizing he had been tricked.

"Let's get going!" shouted Robin. "He looks mighty mad."

"Never fear, Robin," laughed Little John, "his majesty is about to lose something else!" As he spoke the coach wheels fell off. Little John had also been busy!

When he returned to the castle, Prince John was beside himself with rage.

"S-s-so s-s-sorry, S-s-sire, I s-s-saw the trick, but . . ." said Sir Hiss.

"Silence, slithering scoundrel! My fortune is lost, but not for long. Sheriff, raise the taxes! Bring me all the money in this wretched town," Prince John snarled, cruelly. "I shall have my revenge."

That very day, in another part of the town, it was little
Skippy Bunny's birthday. His sisters had saved all year long
to give him a shiny new gold coin.

"Happy birthday, Skipp!" came a gruff voice suddenly
from the doorway. The wicked Sheriff of Nottingham had
come to call.

"Surely such a greeting deserves a little something in return," said the Sheriff to the astonished bunny as he snatched the coin. Then he was gone, slamming the door behind him.

Skippy took one look at the empty box and began to cry.

Little Skippy's ears pricked up when he heard another *rat tat tat* at the door.

"Alms for the poor! Alms for the poor!" cried a poor, blind beggar man.

"Oh, kind Sir, how we would like to help," said Mother Rabbit, "but I am a poor widow and . . ."

"Say no more," interrupted the beggar, removing his spectacles. "I bring you gold, and for little Skippy, here is a bow, some arrows, and a hat, just like mine."

Skippy and his sisters let out a cry of joy. "Yippee, it's Robin Hood! Hurray, Hurray for Robin!!"

The Sheriff was still busy collecting taxes. His nose was so long, he could sniff out gold coins no matter where they were hidden. He burst into the blacksmith's house.

"Okay Smithy, hand over the loot," he said, pulling on the poor hound's plaster cast. "Upsy-daisy!"

When the Sheriff tipped up the blacksmith's cast, several gold coins clattered to the floor. The Sheriff whisked them away as taxes.

A little later that day, Skippy was testing his new bow. But as luck would have it, his first arrow landed right in the middle of the castle courtyard.

"Don't go, Skippy!" cried his friends. "Prince John will kill you." But Skippy was already sliding under the portcullis. He was almost as brave as Robin himself.

"On guard, little bunny!" called a hen. "Are you friend or foe?" Skippy had been spotted by Lady Kluck.

"Oh, don't tease him, Klucky," scolded Maid Marian gently. "He wears Robin Hood's hat—he must be a friend."

Skippy took his arrow and returned to his friends.

Maid Marian and Lady Kluck, her lady-in-waiting, shared a very special secret. Once inside the castle, Marian unfolded a picture of her beloved Robin Hood.

"Oh Klucky, if only Robin and I could marry, but with King Richard away it's quite impossible," said Maid Marian, sighing. "Do you think he has forgotten me?"

"Why no, Milady," reassured Lady Kluck. "Robin could never forget you, and one day, very soon, he will return to marry you."

At that very moment, back in Sherwood Forest, Robin was thinking of the kind Maid Marian. "Oh, Little John," he sighed, "such a high born lady as Maid Marian could never marry an outlaw."

But Little John had other things on his mind. "Cheer up Robin," he said. "What you need is a bowl of my soup."

"Did I hear someone mention soup?" asked Friar Tuck, stepping into the clearing. He slurped a spoonful from the pot. "M-m-m-m! Delicious." Friar Tuck cleared his throat. "Friends, I bring good news. There is to be a Tournament of Golden Arrows in Nottingham to judge the best archer in the Kingdom, and the judge will be Prince John!"

The great day had come at last. What a Tournament it would be! Archers from all over England began to gather in Nottingham. Soon there was such a crowd that some climbed into the trees for a better view.

The fanfares sounded, and the drums rolled. Soon the Tournament of the Golden Arrows would begin.

And as for the prize, it was to be a kiss from the lovely Maid Marian!

A kiss from Maid Marian!! Robin Hood just *had* to win the Tournament. He didn't know that clever Prince John had devised the tournament as a trap.

Robin Hood and Little John put the finishing touches on their disguises.

"Well I swear, Robin," said Little John. "Not even your mother would know you dressed like that!"

"You don't look so bad yourself, Little John," replied Robin. "Whoops! Sorry Milord, I meant to say Sir Reginald, Duke of Chutney!"

Little John made straight for the royal box and was warmly welcomed by the Prince.

As for Marian, she secretly hoped that her beloved Robin was somewhere in the crowd.

But sly old Hiss smelled a rat. "Duke of Chutney, my hat," he said. "I can s-s-see through your phony disguise."

"Back in the basket, Hiss," snapped Little John, and the sulky snake pretended to obey.

"Hmmm . . . if Little John is here, that rascal Robin can't be far, but I must have proof," thought the snake, and slithering from the basket, he slid into the crowd. When he saw the balloon seller, he had an idea.

Quick as a flash, Hiss slipped into a balloon, and suddenly, the curious reptile could fly! He floated over to the only two archers left in the tournament—the Sheriff of Nottingham and a very skinny-looking stork.

"Of course, it must be him!" thought Hiss. "No one but that rascal Robin Hood has such skill with a bow. I must warn Prince John." And off Hiss floated, just as quickly as he could.

Friar Tuck noticed Sir Hiss floating overhead, and knew he was up to no good. He rushed to the minstrel, Allan-a-Dale, who was wandering about and singing.

"Quick, Allan! We must use your lute to stop Sir Hiss," cried Friar Tuck. With help from Allan's lute string, he sent an arrow soaring into the sky. Hiss landed with a bump.

The Friar placed Sir Hiss into the barrel and closed the lid.

"S-s-stop, s-s-scoundrels! S-s-someone s-s-save me!" cried Hiss.

"Keep hissing, creepy one. No one will hear you now," said Friar Tuck.

43

The Tournament was nearly over and the prize was almost Robin's. But the Sheriff had other ideas. Robin's arrow sped through the air, but Nutsey, the Sheriff's sneaky accomplice, moved the target! Robin, seeing the trick, dispatched a second arrow to redirect the first. The arrow whistled through the air, then hit the target—*ding*! a perfect bull's-eye!

"Bravo! Bravo! Bravo!" cried Maid Marian, overjoyed, for she knew the stork must be none other than Robin Hood himself.

Prince John smiled as the stork approached the royal box.
The best marksman in the kingdom could only be Robin
Hood.

"Advance, brave archer. Your prize awaits!" spoke the
Prince. As Robin bowed, Prince John struck him. The
disguise fell away, and Robin Hood's identity was revealed!

"Guards! Seize the outlaw!"
shouted Prince John. "He shall
hang this very day."

"Have mercy, Prince John!"
cried Maid Marian.

The Sheriff laughed as the guards tied up Robin Hood. "Hah hah! So you thought you had us fooled. But there is justice for traitors!"

"Justice will only be done when King Richard returns," replied the courageous Robin. "Long live King Richard!"

On hearing these words, Prince John started to jump off his throne, but something was holding him back.

"Not so fast, Oh Majestic One!" came a voice from behind. "The Duke of Chutney here, but you can call me Little John!"

"H-e-e-e-l-p!" cried the Prince.

"Stop snivelling, and have the Sheriff untie my friend, or you will die," said Little John, holding a dagger to the Prince's back. So a very unhappy Prince ordered an even unhappier Sheriff to free Robin Hood.

Robin Hood was free, but he was still in great danger. A howling pack of ferocious guards was speeding towards him. "On guard!!" cried Robin Hood, the thought of Maid Marian giving him new strength. He pulled his sword and with amazing skill he fought off his attackers single-handedly.

What a battle! Robin fought bravely, but he was so outnumbered that he was glad to see his friend leap into the fight.

"Take that, you scoundrel!" roared Little John as he landed a punch right on the Sheriff's long nose.

"Oooowww! Oooohhh!" yelled the guards as they were felled one by one.

"Ah revoir, friends," shouted Robin Hood triumphantly. "Better luck next time." Swinging from a rope, he scooped up Maid Marian and disappeared into the forest.

"Oh Robin," she cried, "you're so brave!"

"And you my love, are so beautiful," he replied. "Oh, Marian, please say you'll marry me."

Robin Hood and Maid Marian escaped into Sherwood Forest, where they joined Robin Hood's band of Merry Men in a celebration. They played music and danced long into the night, and they sang this song:

"Even in a land
Where bad conquers good,
There's always a hero,
And his name is Robin Hood!
    And even in a city
Where the sun never shines,
A maiden, oh, so pretty,
Will bring back happy times!

For love conquers all,
Even sadness and pain.
Yes, love conquers all,
And keeps away the rain!"

A little later that night, after much singing and dancing, it was time for a bit of fun with puppets. With some branches, a stuffed shirt and a paper crown, the Merry Men fashioned a likeness of Prince John. A glove with two buttons soon became the horrible Hiss! They put on a skit.

"S-s-sire, why do you s-s-suck your thumb s-s-so?" asked the fake Hiss.

"Boo-hooooo!" cried the dummy of Prince John. "I want my mommy; naughty Robin has stolen all my money!"

Everyone roared with laughter.

Back at the castle, Hiss was in big trouble.

"This will teach you not to be there when I need you," yelled Prince John, squeezing the snake in a strangling hold. Hiss began to turn green.

"Your majesty would be wise not to kill the snake. He may yet be useful," said the Sheriff. "And anyway, I know how to make you very happy indeed! Taxes, lovely taxes—let's raise taxes."

As the Sheriff carried out his ruthless tax campaign, Nottingham's poor became even poorer. Hard times had also come to Friar Tuck's church. The collection box was empty since no one in the town could spare a penny, but Friar Tuck smiled when he saw who had come to visit—the church mouse and his wife.

"We were saving this coin for a rainy day, but the sun no longer shines in Nottingham, so we want you to take it," said the church mouse.

The generosity of his good friends brought tears to Friar Tuck's eyes, as he lovingly placed the coin in the box.

Before long the Friar felt a tap on his shoulder. "Okay Tuck, I've come to collect your taxes," a voice growled. And pushing right past Friar Tuck, the Sheriff seized the collection box and gave it such a shake the coin fell out.

"Just as I thought," said the Sheriff. "I'll take this; the Prince needs it more than you."

Friar Tuck was so angry, he flew at the Sheriff, waving his fist!!

The Sheriff took pleasure in throwing Friar Tuck in prison. That very night, the Friar could be found chained to a wall in the castle dungeon. His unfortunate cell companion, Grandpa Owl, had been imprisoned because he had no money to give Prince John.

"If this goes on," said Grandpa Owl, sighing, "soon all Nottingham will be in prison."

"Exactly!" replied Friar Tuck. "There will be no one left to pay taxes, and . . ."

". . . and the Prince will have to free innocent subjects like you and me," interrupted the owl.

"Free us? You're joking, my good brother," Friar Tuck said. "Prince John would sooner have us executed."

Even as they spoke, Prince John and Sir Hiss were gazing out the castle window at the Sheriff, who was preparing the gallows for Friar Tuck's execution.

"Oh, how happy I am," chuckled the jubilant Prince. "The Friar, in prison. What good news! He will hang at dawn, and when the wretched Robin Hood comes to save him, we will be waiting. What does my Royal Serpent think of that?"

"S-s-sire, your Royal S-s-sovereign is the s-s-slyest s-s-schemer that ever lived," replied Hiss.

News travels fast in Sherwood Forest, and it was not long before Robin heard about Friar Tuck. He quickly disguised himself as a blind beggar and went directly to the castle. As he approached, a royal guard took aim.

"Halt! Who goes there?" squawked the guard, giving Robin a poke with his bow. "Not even Robin Hood himself could get past me and live!"

"Alms for the poor!" cried Robin, "I'm just a poor, blind man."

The guard went on his way and Robin wasted no time. Off came his disguise and he signalled to Little John. Together they crept into the castle and began searching for the Sheriff. They soon found him, sound asleep, on prison duty. Robin stealthily stretched out his hand for the keys fastened to the Sheriff's belt, but the sound of footsteps made him dart back into the shadows.

"Whew! That was close," whispered Little John as a guard stamped past.

Little John jumped the guards from behind, and in no time at all he had them both trussed up like turkeys at Christmas time.

"Here, catch!" whispered Robin, as he threw the keys to his friend. "Set the prisoners free, while I take care of the royal treasure!"

In the royal bedchamber, all was quiet. Prince John, clutching his gold tightly to him, was dreaming of the day when all the money in the world would be his.

Sir Hiss's little cradle gently creaked, and his sharp eyes were firmly squeezed shut. Neither of them stirred as Robin crept silently into the room.

Meanwhile, down in the dungeon, Little John unlocked a
cell. "Cock-a-doodle," whistled Allan O'Dale. "What a sight
for sore eyes. But what kept you? We were beginning to run
out of songs to sing."

Little John unfastened his chains and those of Toby Turtle.

"I was okay," croaked the tortoise. "When I got tired of
singing, I just tucked myself into my shell."

Little John laughed. "Now you are free," he said.

As Little John continued freeing the prisoners, he was greeted by all with cries of joy. "Let me shake your hand, kind Sir," chirped a small bird with a fluffy white beard. But there was no one happier than Friar Tuck. He hadn't been in any hurry to go to heaven!

Meanwhile, Robin Hood had rigged up a rope and pulley to lower the gold to Little John and the Merry Men who were waiting below. Robin had just climbed on the rope himself, when Hiss's eyes flashed open.

"Your Majesty, wake up!" cried the snake. "We've been robbed!"

Try as they might, neither Hiss nor the Prince could reach Robin, but their shrieks woke the archers.

"Ouch! Little John, pull me in. These arrows sure are sharp!" yelled Robin.

With a *whooosh* of the rope, Robin Hood landed safely in Little John's arms. But the friends were still in danger. "Quick!" said Robin. "Grab the gold and run. I'll take care of the Sheriff."

The Friar and Little John wasted no time. Together with the newly freed prisoners, they ran for the drawbridge.

While his friends made their escape, the brave Robin Hood dashed up the stairs of the castle tower, the wicked Sheriff and his band of archers hot on his heels.

"Hah hah hah! I've got you now," roared the evil Sheriff as he hurtled up the spiral staircase. "You can either jump from the tower, or be burnt alive!" The Sheriff's terrible laugh echoed through the castle.

The prisoners climbed into a cart to speed their escape. "All aboard! Full speed ahead!" cried Little John, pulling the cart while Friar Tuck pushed. The rickety cart, piled high with gold, sped across the drawbridge and into the safety of Sherwood Forest.

Robin Hood, after eluding the Sheriff, leaped from the castle wall into the moat. Under a hail of arrows, he swam across and escaped into the forest, too.

The wicked Prince John's plot was foiled!

There was great happiness in Sherwood Forest that night. "Long live Robin Hood!" cried Little Skippy, and everyone cheered loudly.

"Hurray! Hurray for Robin Hood," cried Friar Tuck, "and long live good King Richard! May he soon return to bring justice to our land!" Friar Tuck raised his eyes towards heaven. "May our prayers be answered very soon."

The Friar's prayers were soon answered. A few days later, all the bells in England were ringing to announce the return of King Richard. Tuck had a very important task! He was to ask if Robin Hood could marry the King's niece, the lovely Maid Marian.

"What!" cried King Richard, when he heard the Friar's request. "An outlaw for an inlaw! The very idea! And yet, I have heard such good things about Robin Hood. . . My answer must be yes."

Tuck couldn't wait to tell his friends the good news.

The lovely Maid Marian's wish finally came true. She married her beloved Robin Hood and they both lived happily ever after! The minstrel, Allan-a-Dale, wandered through the countryside, singing of Robin Hood's exploits, and ending with this refrain:

"Robin Hood, Robin Hood,
Riding through the glen,
Robin Hood, Robin Hood,
With his merry men.
Feared by the rich,
Loved by the poor,
Robin Hood, Robin Hood, Robin Hood!"

Published by
Gallery Books
A Division of W H Smith Publishers Inc.
112 Madison Avenue
New York, New York 10016

Produced by
Twin Books
15 Sherwood Place
Greenwich, CT 06830

© 1989 The Walt Disney Company

ISBN 0-8317-7408-8

Printed in Hong Kong

1 0 9 8 7 6 5 4 3 2